STAR WARS®
EPISODE I
JOURNAL

Queen Amidala

Jude Watson

LUCAS BOOKS

SCHOLASTIC INC.

New York Toronto London Auckland Sydney
Mexico City New Delhi Hong Kong

No part of this publication may be reproduced in whole or in part, or stored in a retrieval system, or transmitted in any form or by any means, electronic, mechanical, photocopying, recording, or otherwise, without written permission of the publisher. For information regarding permission, write to Scholastic Inc., Attention: Permissions Department, 555 Broadway, New York, NY 10012.

ISBN 0-590-52101-2

Book designed by Madalina Stefan.

SCHOLASTIC and associated logos are trademarks and/or registered trademarks of Scholastic Inc.

12 11 10 9 8 7 6 5 4 3   9/9 0 1 2 3 4/0

Printed in the U.S.A.

First Scholastic printing, June 1999

Queen Amidala

I am Amidala, Queen of Naboo. I am fourteen years old. I did not get to be Queen by being intimidated.

But my first real crisis is here. And I can admit it only in this journal.

I don't know what to do.

The situation is clear: The people of Naboo are in a stranglehold. The Trade Federation has ringed Naboo with orbiting ships, preventing any supplies from going in or out. Our thriving trade business has been cut off.

Food is scarce. Underneath the eerie quiet in the streets, I sense panic.

The Trade Federation is making an example of us. They pay no attention to the rules of law. And we are caught, helpless, while the Galactic Senate talks and talks and talks.

But if the situation is clear, the reasons for it are not. Why Naboo? That's what I don't understand. Why was the Trade Federation so confident that the Senate would not stop them?

Can it be because they think a young, recently elected queen would not have the strength or cunning to resist them?

I can only ask the question in this journal. A queen should never question her strength aloud. She must assume strength, even when she feels uncertain.

That's why I started the journal. I need a place to ponder possibilities and courses of action. As Queen, I have allies and advisors and counselors. But when it comes to decisions, I am alone. The people will look to me if my decision is wrong, not to my counselors.

Even though I listen to advice, I listen to my instincts most of all. The best way to be in touch with them is by puzzling things out for myself. So my closest advisor is this data pad. It fits in a sleek pouch under my clothes. I don't go anywhere without it. On a peaceful planet, I think of it as a secret weapon.

I've been patient during the blockade. I've listened to my Council of Governors, who all advise me to wait. Palpatine, my Senator, is pleading our case before the Senate on Coruscant. He tells me to be patient, too.

But I've never been good with patience. For close to a month I've waited while the Senate has debated. I am no longer willing to wait.

Just a few days ago, I contacted Valorum, Supreme Chancellor of the Senate. I told him that I am holding him personally responsible for the suffering of my people. Every day he delays he takes bread out of the mouths of the starving children of Naboo.

I must say, Valorum turned pale. I could tell from his hologram that I'd shocked him. Fine with me. I'd meant to.

At least he *did* something. At this very moment, Jedi ambassadors are meeting secretly with the Federation's viceroy, Nute Gunray. That foul Neimoidian deserves to be taught a lesson. When the Chancellor calls on the Jedi, he means business. The Federation should crumple like dry leaves.

But I should have heard by now. It's time to learn what progress has been made.

LATER

For official communications, I always put on my ceremonial robes and powder my face dead white. I paint my lips red and add the red scar of remembrance that splits my lip. It is a Naboo ruling tradition, older than memory, that marks a time of suffering for Naboo, before the Great Time of Peace.

The official trappings are not only a mark of respect to my predecessors. They're a shortcut to instant authority. When you're as young as I am, you use everything you've got.

Here on Naboo, we elect our rulers democratically. At first, when I announced my intention to run, people scoffed at me. Who is this girl, they said, the daughter of humble farmers? Why should we put our fate in her hands? Even if King Veruna is corrupt, should we trust a child to rule?

They ignored the fact that from an early age, I had been trained by the best teachers on Naboo. They ignored the fact that I had served as ruler of Theed, our capital city, for two years, and could best King Veruna in any debate. And they ignored the fact that I love Naboo with every cell in my body.

Soon, they could not ignore these facts anymore. As I traveled the cities and towns of Naboo, speaking and listening, the people did something extraordinary: They gave me their trust. They began to brag about my age instead of mocking it. King Veruna was ousted, and I was elected by an overwhelming majority.

I asked for their faith, and they gave it. I can't let my people down.

I decided to conduct the communication to Nute

from the formal throne room, with Sio Bibble, Governor of Theed, and Captain Panaka, head of the Royal Security Forces, by my side.

It was the first time I'd directly contacted Nute since the start of the blockade. My strategy was to infuriate him by treating him as though he wasn't important.

Nute appeared on the view screen. I can't say I find the Neimoidians a handsome race. Their skin is a dull greenish color that absorbs no light. Their eyes are an alarming yellowish orange. But even a Neimoidian, I'd guess, would never call Nute handsome.

"Again you come before me, Your Highness," Nute said. "The Federation is pleased."

Pleased? Did he take me for a fool? It wasn't hard to see the contempt beneath his oily diplomatic phrases. It made me furious.

Wait, I told myself. One thing I've learned is not to let contempt bother me. It means my opponent thinks he's smarter than I am.

Once upon a time, King Veruna thought that, too. Now he's farming rocks in the Naboo Wastelands.

"You won't be pleased when you hear what I have to say, Viceroy," I told him. "Your trade boycott has ended."

His smug smile didn't falter. He said he was not aware of such a failure.

I shot back that I was perfectly aware that the

Chancellor's ambassadors were there. Nute had been commanded to reach a settlement.

To my surprise, Nute didn't budge from his position. He said he knew nothing about any ambassadors.

I took a beat to study him. He was lying, of course. He must be. Jedi do not fail.

I told him to beware. The Federation has gone too far this time.

He replied that he would never do anything without the approval of the Senate. But something rang false in his words. I felt as though I was in a mist, and couldn't see ahead. But one thing I was sure of: The Senate would never approve the actions of the Trade Federation. I had to depend on that.

There was nothing to be gained by listening to Nute's lies, so I cut the communication short and turned to my advisors.

Governor Bibble looked nervous. He thought Nute Gunray seemed unconcerned about the ambassadors . . . which meant Nute must have something dire up his sleeve.

I half-listened to Bibble. I was already one step ahead of him. I am usually one step ahead of Bibble, but I still value his opinion. He is someone I can trust.

It wasn't always that way. Bibble had been one of my rivals when I ran for ruler of Naboo. He dismissed me, at first. He was one of those who said I was too young.

But Bibble's opinion has transformed from casual dismissal to cautious respect to genuine loyalty. I feel the same for him. He would make any sacrifice for Naboo, just as I would.

I didn't want Bibble to know that I was just as worried as he was. When the Queen looks worried, rumors get started, and people's faith is shaken. I gave an order to reach Senator Palpatine.

I was relieved when Senator Palpatine's kindly face appeared on the view screen. Quickly, I told him that there was no sign of the ambassadors.

Palpatine's welcome changed to a frown. He was mystified. He had received assurances that the Jedi had already arrived.

Then suddenly, the hologram began to waver, and his communication was cut off. I could only catch the words "message" and "negotiate."

Captain Panaka looked grave. The Federation could have jammed our communication. That was a bold step. Immediately, Bibble jumped to conclusions and shouted, "Invasion!"

I was barely able to keep my irritation in check. He was overreacting. He had to be.

Captain Panaka agreed with me. He couldn't imagine that the Federation would take such a step.

Punishment from the Senate could be severe. The Senate could stop the Federation's business cold by preventing them from trading with any planet in the Galactic Republic. And Neimoidians are more interested in trade than war.

So why were they risking so much?

I made a decision. The only thing we could do was delay. We had to wait for the Senate to act. We must continue to negotiate.

Bibble was nervous. Panaka was grave. Bibble pointed out that negotiation would be difficult without a communications system or ambassadors. This is why I like him. I can count on him to point out the obvious, just when I don't want to hear it.

I knew Bibble had a point. Why should we negotiate, when the Federation had made it clear that they had only contempt for our laws and the laws of the Senate? And Captain Panaka was right when he pointed out that an invasion could be disastrous for Naboo. We have many advantages from our generations of peace. But along with that comes a people unused to war and a small security force — well trained, but no match for the droid army of the Federation.

"I will not allow any actions that could lead to war," I said finally.

Naboo has thrived and prospered during the Great

Time of Peace. Maintaining that peace is an obligation that has been passed down from ruler to ruler for generations. I would never let anything jeopardize that. The consequences for my people would be disastrous.

I left the throne room and went to my private chambers. I stood looking out over the city of Theed. My city.

I have a reputation for wisdom, and it's been hard-earned. My secret is simple. You learn the most by silence. If you stay silent, if you watch instead of act, others reveal truth. Even liars end up revealing more than they want to. Add this to the respect you automatically receive from some fairly complicated ceremonial robes, and you can do right by your people and your world.

I leaned my forehead against the cool window. Below, the great waterfalls of Theed sparkled. Trees and plants surrounded the square in a thousand shades of living green. My planet is a jewel. From deep space, it looks like an emerald. It is a world that I love. I would die before I see my people hurt, my world destroyed.

But am I choosing the right way to protect it?

I have failed. The Federation has invaded Naboo.

It started at dawn. We were unprepared. Of course we were unprepared! We have not had war on Naboo for many lifetimes. The last war scarred our memories. We vowed then that peace would never die.

The reports trickled in. Battle droids landed in huge armies and marched into the towns. They herded up people and forced them into camps. Many people resisted, but the armies overpowered them.

I can see the invaders now from the palace window. My people are confused, crying, shouting. A battle droid just blasted a woman who dared to question it.

I must be strong. I have to keep a clear head. They will be here soon. After they have taken away anyone who can help us. After they have destroyed all resistance. Then they will come for me. But the Queen they find won't be the Queen they want. Even though I've fought the idea, it's time to follow through with Captain Panaka's plan.

I am Amidala, Queen of Naboo. But I am also Padmé, handmaiden.

I've called one of my handmaidens to my chambers. Her name is Sabé. She is exactly my height and has brown eyes, like me.

She's the perfect decoy.

The Queen's handmaidens are an elite group. They aren't servants, or pretty decorations for the court. They are chosen for their courage and intelligence, and are highly trained in defense. They would give their lives for the Queen and for Naboo.

In other words, they aren't there to fetch me glasses of nectar. Sabé is the bravest and cleverest of all my attendants. She is also my best friend.

When I became Queen, one of my first meetings was with Captain Panaka to discuss security. He told me that the handmaidens were chosen to be near to my height and weight. Should any danger arise, each of them is prepared to take my place. To be my decoy.

I argued with him. One of my duties as Queen is to accept any danger that might arise from my position.

"This is not a choice of yours!" Captain Panaka said. "This is an established security procedure."

Finally, we agreed to stop the argument. After all, Naboo had been at peace for some time. What danger could possibly threaten the Queen?

Now, here it was, a larger threat than we could ever have imagined. And though I am prepared to face a thousand droid armies, I have to stop and ask myself what is best for Naboo. My capture could hurt my people. If they know I've escaped, it could bring them hope. And I could work to free them.

I called for Sabé, and she entered silently. We just looked at each other for a moment. Tears glittered in her eyes but didn't fall. On her face was written the same sorrow that was written on mine. The same sick anger. Through the thickness of the palace walls, we could hear the sounds of the droid army and their merciless march into our beloved city.

"It's time," I told her. "I have to ask of you something I have no right to ask. Posing as Queen will put you in grave danger."

She didn't flinch. She took one look out the window, at the battle droids ringing the square.

"I am ready for whatever happens, Your Highness," she said quietly.

"Padmé," I corrected softly. We exchanged sad smiles.

We barely had time to paint her face white and her lips crimson. I brought out an impressive cloak with black feathers and Sabé slipped it on. Perfect.

Then I slipped off the amulet I always wear around my neck. My parents gave it to me when I left to take on the Governorship of Theed. It's a stone my father found on our land. My mother fashioned the clasp.

The amulet means everything to me. All the love and protection my parents gave to me is concentrated into that smooth stone. I told Sabé to wear it.

Sabé took a step back, already shaking her head. She knew what the amulet meant to me. But I insisted.

"Take it," I said. "It's all I have to give."

I pray it will protect her. I'll wear it again when Naboo is free.

LATER

I have slipped into the more simple dress of Padmé. Battle droids are outside in the hallway.

Nute Gunray himself is here. He requires the Queen's presence in the throne room.

I am ready. I don't know when I'll be able to record my next entry. Or where I'll be.

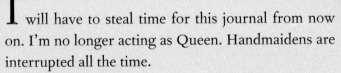

I will have to steal time for this journal from now on. I'm no longer acting as Queen. Handmaidens are interrupted all the time.

I am aboard the Queen's transport ship. How I got here is still incredible to me.

But let me start at the beginning.

The battle droids escorted us to the throne room, where Viceroy Nute Gunray waited. With him were Sio Bibble, Captain Panaka, and four of his officers. Nute stood in the middle of the room with his sidekick, Rune Haako.

I had coached Sabé on what was to come. I could guess everything that Nute would say. He was not clever. He went by the book. Eventually, he would resort to threats.

"I brought you here for a purpose, Queen Amidala," he began.

"I was not *brought*," Sabé said, her voice slashing like a sword. "This is my throne room. I do not recognize your authority, Nute Gunray."

Score one for Sabé! I kept my head down so that Nute couldn't see the satisfaction in my eyes.

Nute looked furious. He flourished a paper and told Sabé she had to sign a treaty that would legitimize the Federation's occupation. He has been assured that the Senate will ratify it.

Assured by whom? I wondered. Or was Nute bluffing?

Sabé told him icily that she would not cooperate. Nute didn't seem concerned.

"I think you will when you see what we have in store for your people, Your Highness." He drew nearer, pushing his dull green face close to hers. Sabé didn't flinch. "I hear that the Queen is compassionate as well as wise. She does not like to see suffering."

"Do what you will. I will never surrender!" Sabé spit out the words.

Good, I thought. Her tone was exactly as contemptuous as mine would be.

Nute turned away, making a show of being bored. He waved a hand at the droids and told them to take us to Camp Four.

We were forced from the palace into the plaza. Usually, it is bustling at this time of day. People taking in the air, fruit sellers, and musicians. They were in camps now, and the plaza was filled with tanks and battle droids. The fury in my chest multiplied and rose until I could feel it as a bitter taste in my mouth.

We marched past the tanks, toward the side of the plaza. The silence of the city pressed against my ears. I could hear the hum of tanks, the buzz of STAP fighters overhead. The sounds of an occupied city.

Within me, frustration and sorrow battle with guilt. Is this my fault? Have I been naive?

I tell myself that blame will only slow me down. And in the end, no matter what I could have done or didn't do, it doesn't matter. It *is* my fault. I am Queen.

I make this vow here. I will never be unprepared again.

We turned a corner into a narrow street off the plaza. Suddenly, two men appeared, seemingly out of nowhere. One of them was powerfully built, with a rugged face and clear, piercing blue eyes. The shorter man was younger and slender. They held themselves at ease, but I felt the power in their stillness.

Then a froglike head appeared over the taller one's shoulder. To my surprise, it was a Gungan. A very nervous Gungan. Quickly, he ducked back again.

The tall man spoke first. He asked Sabé if she was Queen Amidala of the Naboo.

The droid sergeant motioned to the battle droids and ordered them to clear the men away.

Suddenly, the two men drew lightsabers from beneath their robes. They cut down the battle droids as if they were carving up dinner.

The battle droid sergeant was the only one left standing. He hesitated, then turned and began to run.

The powerful man lifted a hand. The droid stumbled backward as if pulled by an invisible hand. Then, almost casually, the man dispatched him with the lightsaber.

This was all done in the space of two heartbeats.

"Wowsa," the Gungan breathed.

The tall man introduced himself as Qui-Gon Jinn and his companion as Obi-Wan Kenobi. I'd already guessed who they were — the Jedi ambassadors.

It was quickly decided that someone must go and alert the Senate. First, we had to find transport. Battle droids were everywhere, but Captain Panaka led us toward the hangar by a route of twisting back alleys.

At least fifty battle droids were guarding the ship, but Qui-Gon said it wouldn't be a problem.

Captain Panaka threw him a look, somewhere between respect and disbelief. I had heard of Jedi, of course, but I had never met one. Qui-Gon's calmness in the face of great odds sent a jolt of hope through me.

Unless he was crazy, of course.

I had expected that the Jedi would leave Naboo alone to contact the Senate. But to my surprise, Qui-Gon told the Queen that she should go to Coruscant with them. Of course, Sabé refused.

"They will kill you if you stay," Qui-Gon said. I could see in his eyes that he was not trying to scare the Queen. He was stating something he knew as fact.

"They wouldn't dare!" Sio Bibble protested.

"They need her to sign a treaty to make the invasion legal," Captain Panaka added.

I heard the opinions of my advisors, but I kept my eyes on Qui-Gon. He registered what they said, but his gaze remained steady on the Queen.

"There is something behind all this, Your Highness," he told Sabé. "I'm troubled by the illogic of the invasion."

So am I, I thought.

"My feelings tell me that they will destroy you. Then they can appoint another ruler who *will* sign the treaty."

I was taken aback. Sabé hesitated.

Sio Bibble told the Queen that she must go. Captain Panaka insisted that it was too dangerous. Sabé turned to her handmaidens. Her gaze rested on me for a beat longer. *Command me*, she pleaded.

Captain Panaka was brave and wise. I had often depended on his advice. But the Jedi's words rang true.

If I left, it would look as though I was running away. The Federation could use that. They'd say that I was a coward who abandoned my people for the sake of my own safety.

But if I stayed, what could I do? Fight a hopeless battle against great odds?

No. I will have to leave behind everyone I love. I will have to travel far, even as they are herded into camps like animals. My friends, my parents . . .

I will have to find a way to bear that pain.

I met Sabé's gaze. "We are brave, Your Highness," I said, which told her, *Go!* I felt a stab of anguish, as if my heart had cracked in two.

LATER

To continue: I saw my first real battle in the hangar.

Battle droids were guarding the Naboo pilots. We would need one of them to fly the transport. Without a flicker of concern, Obi-Wan quietly said he would free them.

23

I signaled Sabé with my eyes, and she chose Eirtaé, Rabé, and me to leave Naboo with her. Yané and Saché are to stay behind. They are the youngest and newest in my service. I pray they'll be safe with Governor Bibble.

Qui-Gon told us to keep on walking, no matter what. We strode purposefully toward the Queen's transport. At first, our boldness confused the guards. Meanwhile, Obi-Wan headed for the captured pilots and crew.

I couldn't imagine how we would be able to escape this number of battle droids, but I kept on walking. Heart pounding, eyes front.

Then we were challenged by a battle droid. Qui-Gon answered him politely, but never stopped walking. The droid announced that we were under arrest and drew his blaster.

I didn't get a chance to take a breath. The battle droid was suddenly a heap of metal and parts on the floor. Qui-Gon never broke his stride.

But the other droids were alerted now, and they rushed at him. Qui-Gon's lightsaber was a blur of light and motion. One after another, the droids were dismembered and dismantled. We ran toward the transport while Qui-Gon deflected battle fire.

Meanwhile, Obi-Wan cleared the guards from

around the pilots, his saber cutting through them, slashing, attacking. The pilots ran for the ship.

The battle was over before it had begun. Two Jedi against that many droids! I still can't believe it, and I was there.

Alarms began to sound. We managed to board as more droids entered the hangar. We took off amid heavy fire. I just had time to see Sio Bibble being captured as the transport rose and fired out of the hangar with Ric Olié at the controls.

But we weren't safe yet. There was still the blockade to deal with. We had a spinning, dodging, whirling ride through heavy fire. Stuck in the Queen's quarters, I couldn't monitor what was going on in the cockpit. It was maddening. Once, the power flickered, and we thought we were lost. But apparently one of the droids saved us by reactivating the defense shields.

The ship is on a steady course now. We're outside the Naboo system. I have to stop myself from running to the cockpit and ordering them to take me back. When I close my eyes, I see battle droids bursting into my parents' home. I see tanks in the city of Theed. I see blood in the fountains, and children wearing stunned, blank looks.

But there's no going back. I have to live with this decision. The consequences are mine.

I've received intensive training. I've studied galactic history and culture, governmental philosophy, and military strategy. Sometimes my eyes burned and my head felt as though it would explode. And I thought, with all that training, I was prepared to be Queen.

But nothing has prepared me for this.

So I open my eyes. I swallow against the sickness inside. I take that helpless, blinding fury and I turn it into resolve. I will defeat them. I will see my enemies surrender.

Next stop, Coruscant. I must think of strategies and plans now, because —

LATER

I spoke too soon. Qui-Gon, Obi-Wan, Captain Panaka, and Ric Olié have informed us that our hyperdrive is leaking. We don't have enough power to reach Coruscant. We must land on a planet called Tatooine for repairs.

Sabé nodded in agreement. I wanted to scream. A delay now could cost many lives!

We don't have a choice, they say. Tatooine is apparently our best bet. It is remote, beyond the reach of the Trade Federation. But it is ruled by gangsters and thieves.

Naturally, Captain Panaka is worried. He thinks

that we should find another planet to land on. But Qui-Gon wants me to trust him. Again.

Nothing against Qui-Gon. But from now on, I won't even trust a Jedi. If a landing party leaves this ship on Tatooine, I'm going with them.

Now that I am Padmé, the Queen can command me to perform tasks. I told Sabé she must do this, or it will look suspicious. But does Sabé get just a little pleasure out of telling me to clean up an astromech droid?

Maybe. She's only human. Actually, once I began, I didn't mind the task. I like working with my hands. It takes my mind off the impatience. And after all, the droid saved my life.

Its number is R2-D2. Apparently it stayed outside on the ship's hull, working to fix the deflector shields under heavy fire. I cleaned off the soot and fire residue, then went to work with a polisher. The R2 unit hummed under my hands.

"You deserve a good buffing," I told him. "Good work."

He beeped happily at me.

Suddenly, we heard a loud "Hidoe!" The noise scared us, and we both jumped.

It was the Gungan, Jar Jar. He's the first Gungan I've seen up close. It's so strange that we share a world. I suppose since the Gungans are swamp dwellers they need amphibian features to survive. The Gungan has a billed mouth like a duck and long, drooping ears. He has a long tongue he's fond of slurping outside his mouth, as if he's testing the air.

He handed me the oilcan and introduced himself — a friendly gesture. "Wesa almost to Tatooine planet," he told me. He leaned closer. His hooded eyes were sympathetic and sorrowful. "Mesa berry skeered."

I was taken aback. We were taught to think of Gungans as barbarians. But this one was as gentle as a child. I patted his cool, rubbery hand. I told him I was sure that everything would be all right.

"Mesa notso," he said with a sigh.

I hid my smile. Although we share a world, the Naboo and Gungans do not mix. Most Naboo think the

Gungan race is beneath them. So it interested me to be face-to-face with one. Or should I say face-to-snout?

If I'd met a Gungan as Queen, I might have drawn my most imposing manner around me like a shimmering robe. But as Padmé, I was charmed.

I can't help it. I like him.

LATER
MOS ESPA SPACEPORT, TATOOINE

They left without me! I should have foreseen this. Why should they alert a handmaiden when they were ready to leave? I had to run to fetch Captain Panaka and have him take me to them.

We caught up with them a short distance from the ship. Panaka told them that the Queen had personally asked if I could go along. I could see that Qui-Gon was annoyed, but he nodded. I knew he would accept it. I am good cover for him. With Jar Jar, Artoo, and me, he won't look threatening.

The planet of Tatooine is totally unlike Naboo. My planet is full of green vegetation and blooming flowers. Our rivers and streams run clear and sweet, tumbling into waterfalls as delicate as lace.

Tatooine is dust. Dust, and blinding heat from the two suns overhead. There is no vegetation to speak of, only rocks. The rocks form deep canyons, which rise around you and sometimes block the sky.

Who would choose such a planet to live on?

I got my answer when we reached Mos Espa: criminals and renegades. Strange creatures from all over the galaxies sat in the cafes lining the streets, gambling and shouting. The noise, combined with the heat, made me feel dazed. The streets were narrow and crammed with braying banthas and various other life-forms. None of which, I should add, I had any inclination to get to know better.

Jar Jar was terrified. He stuck close to Qui-Gon, practically walking on his heels. I was nervous myself. But I was also interested. I haven't seen many of the worlds away from my own. This one is so different. Noisy, dusty, dangerous — it is all those things. But it is also crammed full of life.

Qui-Gon told me the planet is controlled by Jabba the Hutt, probably one of the nastier characters in the galaxy. The deserts are notorious for scavengers, mostly Jawas. The permanent dwellers are moisture farmers. They are the ones with a hard life, because they're honest.

"The few spaceports like this one are full of people who don't want to be found," he said.

"Like us," I pointed out.

Qui-Gon gave me a fleeting look of respect. "I suppose." Then his eyes returned to sweeping the street. He's a man who gives off an aura of deep calm. Yet his is the most alert presence I've ever experienced. I feel safe with him.

We stopped in a small plaza. A group of shabby junk dealers huddled around us. A few of the larger shops made an attempt to be presentable. At least it looked as though you wouldn't take your life in your hands by walking through the door.

Qui-Gon pointed to a smaller, more disreputable-looking shop.

I bit my lip to stop myself from rapping out, "No." Amidala would have argued with him. But Padmé lets the little things go.

This isn't the first time it's occurred to me that Padmé is sometimes smarter than the Queen.

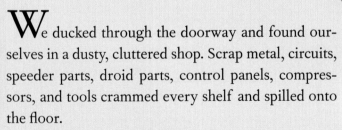

We ducked through the doorway and found ourselves in a dusty, cluttered shop. Scrap metal, circuits, speeder parts, droid parts, control panels, compressors, and tools crammed every shelf and spilled onto the floor.

Suddenly, a fat little blue creature with buzzing wings flew at us. He demanded something in a grating language I didn't recognize.

Qui-Gon told him that he needed parts for a J-type 327 Nubian. At the prospect of a sale, the blue creature immediately became polite and offered any help he could.

He called out harshly in his strange language, and a boy appeared. The boy was slight and dressed in rough garments. He also looked as though he could use a bath. But his piercing dark eyes beamed a fierce curiosity, giving him a look of intelligence.

Qui-Gon and the shop owner spoke for a moment. Then the blue creature took Qui-Gon and Artoo out back to look at parts. I was left in the store with the boy and Jar Jar.

I wandered around, looking at the goods. I couldn't imagine what someone would want with such junk. The boy sat on the counter. He took out a rag and began to clean a metal object. I saw that he was sneaking glances at me at every opportunity. Perhaps the stout blue creature had told him to watch out for shoplifting. His stare was unnerving, more like a man's than a boy's.

"Are you an angel?" he asked me suddenly.

I turned, surprised, and asked him what he meant.

"Deep-space pilots talk about them," he said. "They live on the moons of Iego, and they're the most beautiful creatures in the universe."

Beautiful? I spend so much time trying to appear dignified. I don't think too much about beauty. To tell the truth, when people refer to me as beautiful, I am usually dressed as Queen Amidala. And you can't take a compliment seriously if you're a queen. Everyone flatters you. Everyone wants something. Only a fool would listen.

But I have to admit I was pleased by the compliment of this funny boy.

He told me he listened to the talk around him. Space pilots and pirates and traders visited the shop. He kept his ears open.

"And someday," he said with great conviction, "I'll fly away from here, too."

I asked him if he was a pilot. He seemed very young to fly.

He told me that he'd been a pilot all his life. I tried to hide my smile. I wanted to tease him, to ask if he piloted a speeder when he was a baby, but he was serious. I would hurt his feelings, I thought. So I asked him how long he'd lived on Tatooine.

He had lived here since he was three years old. He and his mother had been sold to Watto, the blue creature.

I was so surprised that I blurted out the question. "A slave?"

And I hurt his feelings, after all.

"I'm a person!" he exclaimed. "My name is Anakin."

What a strange place Tatooine is. Farmers who

cultivate water. Pirates and thieves. And boys who are slaves.

Behind me, Jar Jar mistakenly activated a droid. It lurched about, knocking items off shelves. Then it slammed straight into a pile of parts, which clattered to the floor. Anakin called out to Jar Jar to hit the droid's nose.

Jar Jar did so, but looked so scared and comical that Anakin and I burst out laughing. The sound of it was strange to me. It has been so long since I've laughed.

Qui-Gon strode back in the shop and beckoned to me. I hurried after him.

"Did he have the part we need?" I asked anxiously.

Qui-Gon nodded as he withdrew his comlink. "And the Toydarian is charging a fortune for it," he said.

He raised Obi-Wan on the comlink. Was there anything on board we could sell or trade? I could have told him the answer. Only my wardrobe, which would be useless. I never kept anything of real value on the transport. We would load what we needed for travel. But of course we didn't have time to think of such things when we left Naboo.

Another thing I should have seen coming. Another preparation I didn't make.

Qui-Gon slipped the comlink back in his pocket. He must have seen the worry in my eyes.

"Another solution will present itself," he said matter-of-factly. "We will see."

I wish I had his patience. Now we are stuck on Tatooine. No doubt the Trade Federation has sent troops to track me down. Every second we are here puts us in danger, and Naboo remains in chains.

We've got to find a way. I must get to Coruscant, and soon.

Qui-Gon led us back to the market at Mos Espa. I couldn't tell what he was thinking. He scanned the groups of gamblers and arguing pilots. What was he looking for?

When I asked him, he only said tersely, "A way."

Meanwhile, Jar Jar fell behind. We lost sight of him, and it was a mistake. We learned later that Jar Jar was tempted by a display of frogs in a stall. His long tongue snaked out and captured one. What he didn't notice was that the frog was still attached to a wire in order to prevent such thefts.

When the shopkeeper bounded out of the shop, demanding payment, Jar Jar opened his mouth and the frog snapped away. The tension of the wire sent the frog zinging into a bowl of soup, splashing the creature eating it. This creature happened to be one of the more unsavory types in Mos Espa, which is saying plenty. Jar Jar seems to attract bad luck.

The creature attacked Jar Jar. By this time, Qui-Gon and I had heard the commotion. We turned just in time to see Anakin step between the huge, spider-like creature and the Gungan.

Instead of speeding up to help, Qui-Gon slowed. His expression grew keen as he watched Anakin defuse the situation. By the time Qui-Gon, Artoo, and I caught up to them, the creature — a Dug called Sebulba — had moved away in a huff.

Qui-Gon thanked Anakin and gave Jar Jar a warning look.

"Mesa doen nutten!" Jar Jar protested.

"Fear attracts the fearful," Anakin explained. "He was trying to overcome his fear by squashing you. Be less afraid."

I asked Anakin if that worked for him, and he said it did — to a point.

It was a mature view for a boy. Again, I was struck by Anakin's clear mind. *Fear attracts the fearful.*

The wind suddenly picked up. The abruptness and

ferocity of it surprised us. Dust flew into my eyes, making them sting.

Anakin asked us if we had shelter, and Qui-Gon explained quickly that we did, on the outskirts of the city.

Anakin looked worried. It was too far away. We didn't know how fierce the sandstorms could be on Tatooine. We had to come with him to his home.

I looked at Qui-Gon. Even as he hesitated, the force of the wind picked up, driving the sand against our clothes and skin. Jar Jar moaned in fright, and Qui-Gon nodded at Anakin.

I couldn't see the street behind us, or what was ahead. Everything was a blur. As I followed Anakin, I remembered my grandmother telling me, "Fate is a tangle. Follow one thread."

Her name was Winama. She died last year. She wasn't a farmer like her son, my father. She always preferred city life. I lived with her in Theed during my training. She was a weaver.

Those are the facts I can tell you about Winama. But the feelings are something else. How close we were, and how funny she was, and how she gave me the feeling I could do anything.

But she did have a habit of coming out with sayings I never quite understood. She knew it, too. She knew I was impatient with her. She knew that in my head I was asking, *What does that mean?*

I wish I could talk to her now. I wish I could say, *Winama, I think I'm beginning to understand.*

I miss her so much. But if I knew Winama was in a camp right now, I don't think I could bear it.

I drew my hood around me and covered my mouth. I was choking on dust and sand. I closed my eyes to near slits. I had never felt such driving wind before. The storm blotted out the two suns and turned the air into a stinging force. Anakin held my hand firmly, leading us through the howling storm toward safety. And as he did, I had the strange sensation that I had met one thread of my fate.

LATER

Anakin led us to the quarter where the slaves lived. I could just make out the buildings, small and shabby and built out of what seemed to be sand mixed with a harder substance. Stacked on top of each other, the structures looked more like cubbyholes than houses.

Anakin stopped in front of a hut that looked identical to the others. He waited until he was sure we were all together. Then he quickly pushed open the door and urged us through. We ran inside so that the sand wouldn't blow in.

What does the home of a slave look like?

I didn't know what to expect. My first impression was *care*. Someone here had taken a cavelike structure and poured time and love into it. It looked clean and scrubbed. There wasn't much furniture, but it looked sturdy and well kept.

The kitchen was small, with only a few pots for cooking. I could see alcoves that probably led to the sleeping areas.

"Dissen cozy," Jar Jar said in relief. I had to agree.

Anakin called for his mother. An older woman who had eyes with the same piercing quality as Anakin's emerged from an alcove. She couldn't mask her surprise at seeing her hut filled with dusty strangers and a droid.

"These are my friends," Anakin said quickly. "This is Padmé, and . . . and . . ."

Anakin's mother waited, an eyebrow raised. *And why did you bring strangers into our home?* she seemed to say. Since I'd seen what a dangerous world Tatooine was, I didn't blame her.

"They needed shelter," Anakin said, pointing to the window. We could hear the sand pellets hammering against it.

Qui-Gon quickly stepped in and introduced us all. The woman told us that her name was Shmi Skywalker. I didn't get a chance to hear anything else because Anakin dragged me off to his sleeping al-cove. He had turned into a young boy again, anxious to show me his projects.

I must admit, I am impressed. He has fashioned a protocol droid out of stray parts. The droid has no covering yet, and only one eye. But the programming seems sound. Its name is See-Threepio.

"I'm also building a Podracer," Anakin bragged.

Yet it wasn't empty bragging. This boy has talents beyond his years.

When we returned to the main room for the meal, I noticed how often and how warmly Shmi's eyes rested on Anakin. There is love in this house, I can see that. But there's also a certain sadness. Something lurks in Shmi's eyes that I don't understand.

Qui-Gon is watching, too. He watches even more than I do, if that's possible. But he seems to put pieces together. I just sift through them and try to puzzle out the meanings.

What does he see that I don't?

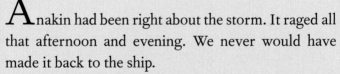

Anakin had been right about the storm. It raged all that afternoon and evening. We never would have made it back to the ship.

As we ate our simple supper, we tried to ignore the wind outside. Over the noise of Jar Jar's slurping, Anakin and his mother tried to give us a picture of what their lives were like. Anakin was cheerful, saying that finding Watto had been good luck. The blue creature was far from kind, but at least he did not beat his slaves.

Shmi had a more hardheaded view of the situation.

As slaves, they were not permitted to travel without permission. They were assigned dwellings. She added that they also have a transmission device implanted in their bodies. If they make any attempt to escape, they will be blown up.

"I don't understand," I said. "Slavery isn't permitted by the Republic. There are antislavery laws —"

Shmi cut me off. "The Republic doesn't exist out here," she said sharply. "We must survive on our own."

I looked at my plate, confused and embarrassed. My life hasn't always been full of riches. I have worked on the land. I have studied and struggled. But now I know that I'd never even glimpsed the kind of hard effort that Shmi faces, just to get through one day.

I have placed all my faith in the Republic. Its laws are formalized, enforced throughout the galaxies. Yet there are places, whole worlds, where they are ignored.

Am I placing too much faith in the Senate? It is all I have. But is depending on it to right the wrongs of the Naboo asking too much?

Anakin broke the silence, asking if I'd ever seen a Podrace. Of course, I hadn't.

Qui-Gon spoke up to say that he had. They are extremely dangerous. Anakin proudly responded that he is the only Human who's able to do it.

Qui-Gon gave him a long look. Again, I had the sense that he was putting pieces together. "You must have Jedi reflexes," he said.

Anakin flushed, pleased. Just then, Jar Jar tried to steal a morsel of food from the communal bowl with his long tongue. In a flash, Qui-Gon reached out and grabbed the end of his tongue. The movement was quicker than the eye could catch. Anakin stared at him, amazed.

And then he asked if Qui-Gon was a Jedi.

"What makes you think so?" Qui-Gon replied.

Anakin told him that he'd seen Qui-Gon's laser sword. Qui-Gon suggested that he'd killed a Jedi and had stolen it.

"No one can kill a Jedi Knight," Anakin said firmly.

A look came over Qui-Gon's rugged face. Rueful. Sad. "I wish that were so."

Anakin told us that he had a dream that he was a Jedi Knight. He returned to Tatooine and freed all the slaves. He asked if that was what Qui-Gon was here to accomplish.

Qui-Gon's smile was sad as he told Anakin that he was afraid not.

Anakin fixed his eager, unblinking gaze on Qui-Gon. "Then why are you here?" he asked simply.

I could see Qui-Gon take a breath and consider. Then he told the truth, or at least part of it. He said we were on our way to Coruscant on a secret mission. We had to land on Tatooine for repairs.

I knew Anakin would burst forth with suggestions and help, and he did. But Qui-Gon pointed out that we needed an expensive part, and Watto was unwilling to trade.

"The junk dealers must have a weakness of some kind," I mused aloud.

Shmi nodded. "Gambling. Everything around here revolves around betting on those terrible Podraces."

Qui-Gon looked thoughtful. "Greed can be a powerful ally."

Anakin almost bounced from his chair in excitement. The big Boonta Eve Classic Podrace was in just two days. He was building a Podracer that Watto didn't know about. The scheme tumbled from him. Qui-Gon could enter the Podracer. He could get Watto to loan Anakin to drive it.

We all stared at the boy. It was actually a good plan. Then I saw Shmi's pale face.

"Annie, you know I don't want you to race," she said quietly. "I die every time Watto makes you do it. It's not just the speed. It's the treachery of those other drivers."

49

"But our friends are in trouble," Anakin insisted.

Qui-Gon's eyes darted from mother to son. He told Anakin that his mother was right. Then he turned to Shmi and asked her if she could think of anyone else who could help us.

Slowly, reluctantly, she shook her head.

"You see?" Anakin cried. "We have to help them, Mom. You always say that the biggest problem in the universe is that no one helps each other."

Shmi turned her face away. I had just caught the sheen of tears. "Anakin, don't . . ."

I felt my heart contract with her pain. I had come from seeing so much suffering on my world. I didn't want to bring any to this house.

"I'm sure Qui-Gon would never want to put your son in danger," I told her. "We'll find another way. There is always another way." I shot an angry look at Qui-Gon. He stared back, impassive. I didn't know what he was thinking.

But Shmi surprised me. She lifted her head. The tears were gone. Or had I imagined them?

"Annie is right. There is no other way," she said. "He can help you. He was meant to help you."

It was a strange thing to say. For a moment, Shmi and I locked eyes. Something passed between us. As though she were giving her son to me. How odd.

THE NEXT DAY

I've spoken to Qui-Gon. I waited until we were alone. Artoo and Jar Jar had gone ahead into the junk dealer's, while Qui-Gon and I were in the plaza.

I started with a question. Was he sure that trusting our fate to a boy we hardly know was the right thing?

"Yes," he said shortly.

"And break his mother's heart?" I prodded.

He turned his neutral gaze on me. "She has willed it."

"The Queen would not approve," I told him.

"The Queen does not have to know," he said.

The arrogance! I couldn't help myself. "Well, *I* don't approve," I snapped.

Perhaps I gave too much away. I don't care. It's so infuriating to be in this handmaiden role, unable to command! Especially when it comes to Jedi. But to be honest, I have a feeling that even if I were in my most stately of costumes as Queen Amidala, Qui-Gon still wouldn't listen to me.

Yes, they are wise and respected and brave. But does anyone ever mention how infuriating the Jedi can be?

Qui-Gon disappeared into Watto's shop. I followed, keeping out of sight. I knew that Qui-Gon must have a plan to deal with Watto. The junk dealer had cunning, but I guessed that Qui-Gon was counting on his greed.

Watto buzzed around Qui-Gon in a flurry of irritation, saying that he'd heard Qui-Gon intended to sponsor Anakin in the Podrace. He pointed out that there was a hefty entry fee. And they didn't take credit, he warned.

Qui-Gon showed Watto a hologram of the ship. He intended to use the ship as the entry fee.

Wait a second, I thought. Qui-Gon was about to gamble with *my ship*?

Qui-Gon told Watto that he had won a Podracer in a bet. Watto's eyes suddenly gleamed with interest. If Qui-Gon would supply the Podracer and the entry fee, he'd supply Anakin, and they'd split any winnings fifty-fifty.

Qui-Gon's eyebrows shot up. If Watto was demanding a fifty-fifty split, then *he* could front the entry fee. If Anakin won, Watto could keep all the winnings, minus what we need for the part.

"And if he loses," Qui-Gon concluded, "you can keep my ship."

My ship? Since when was my ship *Qui-Gon's* ship? My blood boiled. How could he do this without consulting me?

Then I remembered I was Padmé, not Amidala. I couldn't stride forward and give orders. I would have to trust Qui-Gon.

I hate that.

LATER

I am back at Anakin's. He asked for my help fixing the Podracer. I'm afraid this engine is unlike any that I know. But I can hold tools and pass them.

Anakin's friends suddenly appeared to help as well. It's obvious that the little band looks to Anakin as their leader. Even as they tease him for entering his home-built Podracer in such a big race.

Qui-Gon approached us and gave Anakin a battery.

"I think it's time we found out if this thing can run," he said.

I had worked all afternoon. My hands were grimy. I was tired from stooping. And to my eye, it seemed impossible that this makeshift bucket could carry Anakin to victory.

But when I heard the engines ignite and roar, my cheer was louder than anybody's. At that moment, anything seemed possible.

NIGHT

I'm not sure what woke me. I slipped out of bed and went to the window. Shmi sat on the front stoop. She looked up at the night sky. I saw her face in the starlight.

I don't think I've ever seen such sadness.

Is this what life is? Today, we have a victory — the Podracer roars to life. Tonight, that victory cuts someone to the heart.

Is that the bargain we make with life? Does every pleasure have a pain embedded in it, like a stone at the heart of a fruit? The trick is to hold two contradictions at the same time. Pain and pleasure. Exhilaration and sadness. The fruit and the stone.

I don't like contradictions. I like things to be clear.

I'm shivering. It's not from cold, but dread. I had felt safe here. But I was foolish to feel safe.

There are forces out there I don't understand. I do know one thing, though. They want me dead.

There is no safe place. A mother can't protect her child forever. And a queen cannot hide.

THE HANDS OF A BOY

On the day of the race, I woke before dawn. Even before I was fully awake, I was up and hurrying outside. Artoo was painting the Pod. Anakin slept on the ground nearby. He had probably fallen asleep on his feet. Without the light of challenge in his dark eyes, he looked younger. Vulnerable.

I shook my head. What was Qui-Gon thinking? We should be protecting this boy, not depending on him to save us.

I touched his cheek to wake him.

"I was dreaming," he said. "You were leading a huge army into battle."

I couldn't help smiling. I am not a warrior queen, and I can't imagine ever being one. "I hope not. I hate fighting."

I do hate it. And worse, I hate being in exile. How awful that I have to run away, maybe fight one day, just to find peace. That's why I am on fire to get to Coruscant. I want to stand up and say, *This is wrong!* Say it so clearly and strongly that the Senate would rise up and cry it with me. Naboo will be free again.

I told Anakin to hurry. The others had already left for the arena. Today, a race would decide my fate.

Anakin and I rode to the arena together on an eopie, a Tatooine beast of burden. We dragged the Podracer engines behind us. Anakin's friend Kitster rode on another eopie, dragging more parts.

I was shocked at the huge size of the arena and the tremendous crowd. Every available seat was filled. The heat and the noise were like a physical force, pressing against my chest.

"Isn't it great?" Anakin said cheerfully. "The Boonta Classic always gets a crowd. Everyone comes from the Outer Rim Territories."

I saw creatures of every description. Sluglike, spiderlike, tall as trees, tall as my knee. They were all arguing, betting, eating, shouting, fighting, laughing.

"They come because this is the most dangerous race of all," Anakin said, his eyes shining.

I couldn't believe he didn't feel the pressure. This crowd was out for blood. I imagined that a crash or dismemberment would only make them roar with delight and call for more.

Anakin guided our eopies toward a huge hangar nearby. As we entered, I saw Qui-Gon and Watto deep in conversation. I gave Qui-Gon a sharp look. Was there something going on that I didn't know about? He pretended not to notice me. I turned away in frustration.

"This is so wizard!" Kitster called from the other eopie as he surveyed the other Pods. "I'm sure you'll do it this time, Annie!"

This time? I asked Kitster what he meant.

"Finish the race, of course!" Kitster replied.

Shocked, I turned to Anakin. "You mean you've never won a race?"

Anakin looked sheepish. "Not exactly."

"Did you ever *finish* a race?" I persisted.

Anakin threw Kitster a dark look. "I will today," he vowed.

"Of course you will," Qui-Gon said in the calm

tone that made me want to take his lightsaber and clunk him over the head.

We climbed down from the eopie and Anakin and Kitster wandered off.

I've found a quiet place behind the bleachers to write this, but I hear the announcers. The race will begin soon. I must hide my apprehension and wish Anakin luck.

LATER

I didn't have time for much encouragement. Just a few words. "You carry all our hopes," I whispered.

Anakin's gaze was steady. "I won't let you down."

Next to him was Sebulba, the ugly creature who'd almost pummeled Jar Jar. He growled something at Anakin. I assumed it was not in the spirit of good sportsmanship.

"What did he call you?" I asked.

"Slave scum," Anakin replied. "Don't worry, Padmé. He'll be chewing on my exhaust in a couple of minutes."

It was time. I headed to the viewing platform where Shmi was already waiting. Jar Jar stared longingly at the food stalls, unraveling his long tongue as if testing the air for tastes. Then Qui-Gon arrived and took a seat with a calmness I envied.

I turned to him furiously. "This is pure reckless-ness," I said, quietly so the others wouldn't hear. "The Queen —"

Qui-Gon interrupted me with a gesture. "The Queen trusts my judgment. You should, too."

"You assume too much," I fired back. I told him that I didn't see the wisdom of putting our fate in the hands of a young boy.

Qui-Gon looked impatient. "And did the Naboo err when they put their fate in the hands of a girl?" he asked.

He didn't say it to be cruel. But I felt the sting. Did they err? So far, I haven't handled my first crisis very well.

He realized that he had hurt me somehow, though he couldn't have realized why. To him, I'm just Padmé.

"You need to have faith," he said.

I wasn't ready to forgive him. I replied crisply that I only have faith in the things I can see and touch.

"Ah," Qui-Gon said softly. "Perhaps that is your mistake, handmaiden."

Infuriating! He wouldn't speak that way to the Queen.

I hope.

In a nearby box, I saw the biggest Hutt I've ever seen. His body consisted of rolls of undulating fat.

Around him swarmed servants and slaves and nasty-looking hangers-on.

Shmi followed my gaze. "Jabba the Hutt," she observed bitterly. "Proof that no matter how bad it is to be a slave, it could be worse. Jabba could be your master."

"They seem to be waiting for his signal to begin," I said.

"Nothing happens on Tatooine without Jabba's permission," Shmi said, disgusted.

The pilots gunned their engines. Jabba gave the signal.

They were off!

Almost immediately, Anakin stalled. But his engines started again with a roar, and he took off again. But now he is so far behind!

I can't write anymore. Later.

AFTER THE RACE

We watched the distant part of the race on view screens. The track wound through narrow canyons, tall cliffs, high dunes, and flat desert. It was treacherous. I didn't know how anyone could pilot a Podracer at such speeds and survive.

Whenever I caught sight of Anakin, I was amazed at his skill. He swerved, dove, plummeted, corrected, and hopped over other racers. He was one with the machine. He had no time to plan a move — he just *moved*. By the middle of the first lap, he'd regained the distance he'd lost.

Suddenly, I saw a parallel between us. Aren't I moving, swerving, dodging, all without a plan? I am doing things I couldn't have dreamed I could do. Can I, too, regain the ground I have lost?

But now I worried, along with Shmi, about Anakin. Sebulba didn't race fairly. He used any dirty trick he could get away with. Already he had disabled a rival's engine. The driver hit a cliff dead-on in a shattering crash.

No wonder Shmi hates these races. There are no rules!

After the first lap, Sebulba was comfortably in first place. Anakin was in sixth. We cheered wildly as he zoomed past, even though he couldn't hear or see us.

On the second lap, I thought the tension would break me. I wanted to scream, cry, run out onto the track to help Anakin. All of my training in silence and control didn't help with this agonizing tension. The usually calm Shmi was twisting her tunic in her hands until it was a sodden mess. Jar Jar kept up a constant hum of panic.

And Qui-Gon? He sat as if he was enjoying a sunny day! Sometimes, he even closed his eyes. He had risked my life on a nine-year-old's racing skills, and he didn't even break a sweat!

Here is another vow: If I am ever elected Supreme Chancellor of the Senate, I will decree that all Jedi must demonstrate an emotion at least once a year.

Three more racers exploded. We saw the plume of smoke from the last one in the air. Shmi let out a low moan and scanned the view screen. We leaned close, our eyes straining.

Qui-Gon closed his eyes again and breathed.

"There he is!" I screamed the words. Shmi collapsed against me.

For the final lap, Anakin was neck and neck with Sebulba. Our throats were raw with cheering as he zoomed into the arena.

The battle for first place was agonizing. Anakin gained it by faking an inside run, then zooming on the outside. Enraged, Sebulba began to smash his Podracer into Anakin's, beating it relentlessly. Shmi reached for my hand. Anakin's Podracer wasn't built for this abuse. We knew that.

Sebulba gained on the final stretch. Shmi's hand squeezed mine until my bones came together. I didn't even feel it.

Suddenly, Anakin's racer spun out of control. We gasped in terror. But the Podracer smashed into Sebulba's, driving it into a large statue. Sebulba's engine exploded in a fireball. Sebulba was catapulted out as the Podracer crash-landed. He was furious, but was immediately distracted when he realized that his pants were on fire.

Then Anakin burst through the smoke and flame and crossed the finish line.

It was incredible. Amazing. I screamed and laughed and jumped up and down. Not like a queen. Like a girl. At that moment, I was glad to be Padmé. She gives me freedom to do the things that the Queen cannot.

LATER

Even Qui-Gon looked excited. So the Jedi *did* have feelings, after all. We started down toward the hangar. Shmi ran ahead, her eyes streaming tears of joy . . . and relief.

I gazed at the brawling, shouting crowd. Fights were already erupting over bets lost. Winners crowed. Anakin had been a long shot.

"You're just as much of a gambler, Qui-Gon," I said. "Today luck was on your side."

"If you want to call it that," Qui-Gon answered serenely. "Luck is just a word for a force you can't explain." His rugged features softened for a minute. His eyes twinkled. "Something you can't see or touch has just helped you reach a goal, handmaiden. Do you believe in the unseen now?"

I'd just like to know one thing. Why can't you ever get the last word with a Jedi?

When we got to the hangar, Anakin had just returned from being carried around the arena on the crowd's shoulders. His hair was matted and his face was streaked with dirt. He flashed me a joyous grin.

I hugged him close to me and told him I was proud of him. We owe him everything. At last, we could leave Tatooine!

Watto had brought the part we needed to the arena, as he had promised Qui-Gon. There was nothing to keep us here.

Qui-Gon loaded the parts on the eopie's harness. He tied the last knot and turned to me. It was time to go.

The joy faded from Anakin's face. He looked at me, confused. I suppose that he hadn't truly realized that by winning the race, we would leave.

"Can't you stay?" He looked hopeful.

"I'm sorry, Anakin," I said. "We must go. We've stayed too long. I won't forget you."

"Promise?"

"Promise."

I climbed on the eopie behind Qui-Gon. Jar Jar struggled to stay on his. We started off.

Qui-Gon turned to tell Shmi and Anakin that he would be back to return the eopies by midday.

I wanted to turn, too. I wanted to say a last good-bye. I knew Anakin was waiting for me to turn back. But I looked forward. I could feel the girl Padmé slipping away and the Queen taking her place.

Already my thoughts had turned to Coruscant. I was bursting to plead my case before the Senate. To see justice done. To see my people freed.

Padmé would have looked back for a last good-bye.

A Queen cannot.

SOME GREAT EVIL

Location:
QUEEN'S ROYAL
STARSHIP

How long does it take to return two eopies? Qui-Gon has been gone all afternoon.

He must have had another mission to accomplish. That's my guess. If I were Queen Amidala, I'd send for him upon his return and give him a tongue-lashing. I can't trust Sabé to be quite mean enough.

I don't think I can stand being on this planet for one more second. The faces I saw from the palace window on the morning of the invasion cry out to me, urging me to hurry.

I can't stand this. I feel so helpless. We've already

wasted too much time here. It could already be too late. Not to mention that every minute we stay in one location, we place ourselves in danger.

Even the normally inscrutable Obi-Wan looks annoyed. Why is Qui-Gon taking so long? What business could —

LATER

I had to interrupt my griping at Qui-Gon. Anakin burst in. I was so shocked to see him!

He managed to gasp out that Qui-Gon was in trouble. They had met some creature on the way who challenged him. Someone sent by the Trade Federation, I'm sure. Qui-Gon was locked in a deadly battle with him.

We moved fast. Ric Olié took the controls, and we took off. I took a seat in the cockpit. Flying low, we sped over the desert.

At first we could only see a cloud of dust. Then I recognized the strong figure of Qui-Gon. He was battling a dark-caped figure with a horned head. I watched the acrobatic way he moved, the economy and power of his gestures. Any irritation I had ever felt for the Jedi left in a rush.

I am fervently glad that Qui-Gon is on my side.

Qui-Gon must have caught sight of us, though I didn't see him turn his head. Suddenly, he leaped over his adversary. He landed on the ramp outside the ship.

I gasped as the dark-cloaked figure leaped after him. Obi-Wan hurtled out of his seat and ran toward the loading area.

I could only wait, every nerve screaming. Then the comlink crackled.

"He's safe," Obi-Wan said.

I sat rooted to my seat. That brief glimpse of the cloaked figure caused fear, brittle as ice, to strike my heart.

That creature was not some Trade Federation goon or mercenary. Some great evil was working here. Something stronger than I'd imagined. I am sure of it.

Are the stakes higher than even I have feared?

LATER

Sabé has told me that Sio Bibble sent a transmission while I was on Tatooine. He begged me to return to Naboo. The people are starving. The Federation has cut off all food supplies.

Obi-Wan thinks the transmission is a trick to lure me back. Probably. But that doesn't mean my people aren't suffering. I had to wait until everyone was asleep before I sneaked out to the bridge to see the message for myself.

The hologram was grainy and unclear. But Sio Bibble's kind face cut to my heart. Trade Federation trick or not, the suffering on Naboo was written on every feature as he pleaded for me to return.

At least he was still alive.

Worry and anguish filled me. I felt trapped and paralyzed. And tired. So tired.

At that moment, I heard a sound — an echo of the tears locked inside me. I thought I had conjured it from the air, but it was real.

Anakin sat huddled in the corner, trembling. I crossed to him, and he looked up at me with tears in his eyes.

"It's very cold," he said.

I slipped out of my over-jacket and draped it around his shoulders. "You're from a warm planet, Annie," I said. "Space is cold."

But I knew it was more than cold. Qui-Gon's bet with Watto had freed Anakin. He might even be allowed to train to be a Jedi. All of this was good. But he'd had to leave everything he loved behind.

Anakin knew something was wrong in my heart, too. He always seems to know things. "You're sad," he told me.

I chose my words carefully. "The Queen is worried. Everything depends on her appearance before the Senate. She doesn't know if she has the power to change things. I'm not sure, either. I don't know what will happen."

Anakin sighed. "I don't know what will happen to me, either. And I don't know if I'll see you again."

He pulled a pendant out of his pocket and handed it to me. I turned it in my hand. The wood felt smooth and polished. I liked the feel of it in my palm.

"I carved it out of a japor snippet," he said. "It will bring you good fortune."

How funny. Those are almost exactly the words my father used when he handed me my amulet. I fastened Anakin's pendant around my neck. It bumped softly against my breastbone. I touched it, and I felt the same sense of comfort and protection. Anakin has given me something more precious than he knows.

I told him I didn't need a necklace to remember him. Things would change when we got to Coruscant. But my caring for him would always remain.

"I'll always care for you, too," Anakin said. "But I miss —" His voice faltered.

"You miss your mother," I said softly. "When we go forward, we miss the things we leave behind. That's what makes our hearts so full."

A vision rose in my head of my family's farm. Emerald-green fields dotted with yellow flowers. The rich scent of the earth. The strength of my father's hands. The gentle way my mother braided my hair.

I can't lose those things. I won't.

So much lies ahead. So much danger. So much to do. But tonight, I had a moment to comfort someone else. It helped my fear. Maybe the worst fear is when you think you're alone.

Thanks to Anakin, I had a moment of peace. Sometimes, just one moment is enough.

QUEEN

Location:
CORUSCANT

From space, Coruscant sparkles like a star. You think you must be approaching a world of silver and light.

And you are, in a way. The main city of Coruscant long ago spread itself to take in the surrounding countryside. It grew with the wealth and power of the Republic until it covered the entire planet. Streams, rivers, and forests have all been covered over by layers of roads and buildings.

The silver towers flash in the sun. It is a beautiful sight, but not a sight that I am used to.

I thrive on the thousand greens of Naboo. I like to see the rivers run wild, and trees to spread their branches like dancers, and grasses to wave in the breeze.

But Coruscant is the world I must adapt to. It is here that I must make my stand.

When we arrived, Senator Palpatine and Supreme Chancellor Valorum himself met us at the spaceport. I took that as a good sign.

The Chancellor told Sabé that everyone in the Senate was distressed about the situation on Naboo. I hope he means it. He's called for a special session of the Senate so I can present my case.

I had to wait until we reached Palpatine's Senatorial quarters to switch places with Sabé. Here, no one will notice if Padmé disappears. And Sabé will shroud herself and fade into the background.

As Sabé and I changed places, I thanked her for her courage and skill.

"We all need courage now. You most of all," Sabé answered and pressed my hand. There is a fierceness to her quiet ways. Her touch was gentle, but her eyes blazed. "I know you will see us through this, Queen Amidala."

Her faith gives me courage.

I know Sabé is glad to help. But I sensed her relief when she donned her handmaiden's cloak again. I'm relieved, too. At last, I can act. Everything we've done has led to this moment before the Senate.

Senator Palpatine requested an audience so that we could go over strategies. It was good to see him again, and to confer with him. He's always been one of my most trusted advisors. When those on the Council of Governors doubted my abilities, he always backed me. Together, we should be able to sway the Senate.

To my surprise, Palpatine informed me that the Chancellor has been weakened by accusations of corruption. I had thought Chancellor Valorum still held his power base. The news that he is possibly weaker than I thought was distressing.

"The accusations are baseless, but it doesn't matter," Palpatine told me with a worried frown. "It weakens him."

I considered this. Perhaps Palpatine was overestimating the scandal's effects. I asked him what our options could be.

"Our best choice is to push for the election of a new Supreme Chancellor," he said. "Someone strong, an ally. He or she could take control again and force the Senate to act. We would have justice at last."

I didn't like to hear that. Valorum has not been as effective as I would like, but he is still a strong ally for Naboo. "Is there no other way?" I asked Palpatine.

"We could submit the matter to the courts. . . ." he said, his voice trailing off.

That ended it. The courts mean more delay. There's no time left. Naboo is being devastated as I sit here, waiting. I will have to convince the Senate. There is no other way. Everything depends on that.

LATER

Anakin has come to see Padmé. He thinks he will be entering Jedi training, and he came to say good-bye.

He can't say good-bye to Padmé, of course. I could only tell him, as Queen Amidala, that I knew Padmé's heart went with him. He looked so sad when he nodded.

I wish I could have given him a warmer good-bye. I don't know why this boy has become so important to me, but he has.

I've created a division in myself. There is the Queen, and there is Padmé. I am both of them, of course. But I find that I can only be one at a time.

I wonder what it would be like to have no secrets. To be Padmé and Queen, together. Ruler and girl. Mind and heart.

I wore my most regal robes and most complicated headdress. My face was powdered white, my lips deep crimson with the scar of remembrance. I wanted every single Senator to recognize the majesty of Naboo.

The Senate building is enormous, many times bigger than the palace at Theed. Its halls are crowded with people and aliens from many worlds, Senators conferring, aides rushing by importantly, droids rolling by at fast speeds, anxious to complete an errand.

Our little group was made up of Captain Panaka, my two handmaidens Eirtaé and Rabé, and Senator Palpatine. I wasn't nervous. I was ready.

The individual Senatorial boxes are docked at landing bays. When a member is recognized, the box floats to the center of the circular chamber. I saw the elegant white head of Chancellor Valorum in the center box.

Palpatine was still pressing me to call for a vote of no confidence in Valorum. I hoped that after I spoke, the Senate would rise as a body and condemn the injustice of the invasion. A vote of no confidence would not be necessary.

Palpatine began the proceeding by reminding the Senate of the outrageous action of the Trade Federation. Immediately, Lott Dod, the Senator for the Federation, zoomed forward in his box to object. Valorum did not recognize him, and Palpatine was able to continue.

When Palpatine introduced me, I kept my posture perfectly erect, my chin high. I was not pleading. I was *demanding* that they do what was right. Here is what I said:

Honorable representatives of the Republic, distinguished delegates, and Your Honor Supreme Chancellor Valorum, I come to you under the gravest of circumstances.

The Naboo system has been invaded by force. Invaded against all the laws of the Republic by the droid armies of the Trade —

This is where I was interrupted.

Lott Dod objected again. That spindly Neimoidian would not let me get to the end of my statement! He called for a commission to be sent to Naboo to study whether my "accusations" were true.

Accusations!

"Enter the bureaucrats," Palpatine whispered to me. The delegate from Malastare was already calling for the rules of procedure to be obeyed. A commission must be formed.

I held my breath while Valorum consulted with his experts. Then he announced reluctantly that the Federation was right.

"Queen Amidala, will you defer your motion to allow a commission to explore the validity of your accusations?"

Hot rage surged through me. I had never felt such fury. To have come this far, only to be met with more delay! My people are starving — dying — and they want to appoint commissions!

Cool your anger, I told myself. *It should be ice, not heat.*

"I will *not* defer!" I said. "I was not elected to

watch my people suffer and die while you *discuss* the invasion."

I had reached the end of everything. All my hopes. I felt sick inside, and I had to fight against the despair that rose inside me. They wouldn't help me.

I had no choice. There was nowhere else to go. I called for a vote of no confidence in Supreme Chancellor Valorum.

His shock was visible. We locked eyes across the vast Senate chamber. I saw his gaze move to Palpatine. He felt betrayed.

I don't regret it. Palpatine is right. The Senate is mired in its own bureaucratic mud.

Immediately, the chamber filled with excited buzzing. Bail Organa from Alderaan was the first to second the motion. He asked that a vote be taken immediately. Lott Dod once again called for further study.

The Senate erupted. A chant began: "Vote now! Vote now!"

"It appears we have started something," Palpatine murmured to me. "Good."

My gaze swept the quarreling, tumultuous Senate. Yes, we'd started something. We had achieved a strategic victory. But it wasn't the one for which I had come so far, and risked so much.

Palpatine could be right. Change could be the best

thing for the Senate. But change might not be in time to help Naboo.

LATER

I'm back in Palpatine's quarters. I must record an odd conversation I had with Jar Jar.

I stood gazing out over the flashing spires of Coruscant. All that power glittered below me. And yet they could not manage to right one intolerable wrong.

Jar Jar loped up to stand beside me. I could see his reflection in the glass. His large, kind eyes were full of woe. His sympathy seemed like a warm, solid thing. It's strange how I've grown so fond of him.

"Mesa wonder why da guds invent pain?" he asked finally.

"To motivate us, I imagine," I said.

Jar Jar nodded. "Yousa tinken yousa people ganna die?"

"I don't know," I said.

"And da Gungans," Jar Jar said dolefully. "Dey ganna get pasted too, eh?"

I told Jar Jar that I hoped not. Then he said something that surprised me.

"Gungans no die'n without a fight. Wesa warriors. Wesa grande army. Force fields, all dat. Gotta protect wasen ours."

I was preoccupied with my own problems. But Jar

Jar's words cut through them like a knife. I turned to him with new interest, wanting to ask more. But Palpatine entered then. He was full of optimism about the day's events. I saw that he considered the session a great victory.

Captain Panaka informed me that Palpatine had been nominated to succeed Valorum.

"A surprise, to be sure," Palpatine said.

But he didn't seem surprised. Beneath his modesty, I sensed triumph.

Well, why not? Palpatine isn't free of ambition. And it would be good for Naboo to have our former representative as Supreme Chancellor.

I told Palpatine that I feared that even if he were elected, it would take too much time for him to get control of the bureaucrats. In the meantime, Naboo would be destroyed. There was nothing left for me to do here. It was time to return.

Palpatine was aghast. Panaka thinks it's a bad decision, too. They both think I should remain here. Be a queen in exile, waiting for crumbs. Don't they know what kind of Queen I am?

Well, maybe I didn't really know, either. Until now.

If the Senate doesn't condemn the invasion, fear and aggression will rule the galaxies. I will fight against the Trade Federation until my very last breath.

I hear those words, and they surprise me. I've always been an advocate of peace and diplomacy. I don't believe in fighting.

Yet I will fight. Die fighting, if I have to.

LATER
QUEEN'S ROYAL STARSHIP

I am Padmé again. It is not safe for me to remain Queen while traveling. By agreeing to be Queen, Sabé has again pledged her life. After we had changed clothes, we hugged each other, gripping tightly. We both know we may be switching roles for the last time. I might die as Padmé. Sabé might die a queen.

When we got to the landing platform, the Jedi were waiting. The sight of Qui-Gon made my heart lift. Qui-Gon bowed and pledged his continued service to the Queen.

Sabé nodded in gratitude. "I welcome your help. Senator Palpatine fears the Federation means to destroy me."

Qui-Gon's look was resolute. "I promise you, I will not let that happen."

We entered the ship. Ric Olié took his place at the controls. Obi-Wan and Qui-Gon sat nearby. Jar Jar left the cockpit because he was afraid of takeoffs, but he lurked in the corridor in case he was needed. Artoo wheeled into place to monitor the controls. And

Anakin waved at me. I was so glad to see him. I hate to bring him into the middle of a war, but I know Qui-Gon will watch out for him.

On my way to the Queen's quarters, I took a last look back at all of them. What an unlikely group. A Jedi Knight and his apprentice. A Gungan. A droid. A boy.

But they've become my allies. I am glad to be returning home with my friends.

I have a plan.

If I'm going to be a warrior queen, I have to get a running start. I've thought long and hard on this. My enemies are vastly more powerful. They have more weapons. They have more troops. They have everything I don't have. Everything you need for war.

But they do not have something that I have: surprise.

I've called a meeting with the Jedi and Captain Panaka. Sabé and I must switch places again. I need to

86

be Amidala for this. I have a feeling they won't be easy to convince.

LATER

They were impossible. But I won, of course. After all, this is my ship.

It's the same old argument. If I land, I will be captured. If I'm captured, I will sign the treaty. I watched Panaka's lips form the same old words.

I am so tired of being underestimated! Enough. I don't mind being underestimated by the Neimoidians — I can use that to my advantage. But when my own military leader treats me as a figurehead, I want to howl.

I didn't howl.

I said this: *I am going to take back what's ours.*

Qui-Gon said what I expected him to say. As a Jedi, he could only protect me. He could not fight a war for me. Captain Panaka reminded me that there were only twelve of us, as if I couldn't count. He said we had no army, as if I had forgotten that fact.

I ignored them. I turned to the figure who had been slouching against the wall, wondering why he was there, and most likely dying to run away.

"Jar Jar Binks!" I called.

He immediately snapped to, all twitching hands and clumsy feet. "Mesa?"

I would have smiled at him, if I were Padmé. Instead, I only softened my voice.

"I need your help," I said.

LATER

The Federation has spotted us. There is only one battleship in orbit above Naboo. After all, they control the planet. There is no more need for the blockade.

So they know we are here. Within minutes, we will be landing in the Gungan swamp.

The planet looks so peaceful as we approach it from above. There are no signs of war, just the deep greens of forests and meadows and the lovely blues of the seas.

But on this planet lies my greatest challenge. I'll have to summon up everything I've learned and everything I know. I'll have to find every drop of courage I possess. What lies ahead will take everything I am, and ask for more.

I will write again when I can.

THE ALLIANCE

Location:
GUNGAN
SWAMP

We waited at the edge of the Gungan swamp. The dank smell felt thick in my lungs. My feet sank slightly in the mud. The overhanging trees dripped shadows onto the murky surface of the lake.

Jar Jar had disappeared beneath the surface some time ago. He would make the first contact with the Gungans below in the bubble city of Otoh Gunga.

Everyone stared at the spot where he had disappeared. They were all impatient for his return. They were also irritated at the Queen, but couldn't show it.

They had no idea why we'd landed here, or why the Queen had sent Jar Jar below. I didn't want Sabé to reveal my plan until I knew the first part would work. Everything depended on that. I drew my cloak around me and focused my mind on what lay ahead.

Finally, we saw the waters part. Water streamed over Jar Jar's long head. Slowly, he emerged and climbed onto the bank.

"Dare-sa nobody dare," he told us.

"Probably taken to camps," Captain Panaka said.

"Or wiped out," Obi-Wan said, his hand on the holster of his lightsaber.

The disappointment hit me like a blow. But Jar Jar was already shaking his head, his flapping ears flying. He said that the Gungans were probably hiding in their sacred place.

We followed Jar Jar away from the lake, deep into the swamp. He followed no path that I could see. Every so often we heard the buzz of Federation STAPs overhead, but the dense foliage protected us from being spotted.

Jar Jar stopped suddenly in a small clearing. The trees here were enormous, with thick, twining roots like huge snakes slithering against the dark earth.

He lifted his head and made an odd, chattering sound. A second later, Gungans appeared out of the forest, riding kaadu.

Jar Jar greeted an officer as Captain Tarpals. The captain did not look overjoyed to see Jar Jar.

"Wesa comen to see da boss," Jar Jar told him.

The captain cast an extremely unfriendly eye over all of us. "Mebbe ouch time for all-n youse," he muttered.

"Ouch time" didn't sound like a good sign. The Gungans formed an escort on either side of us. We walked even deeper into the swamp. Now the overgrowth blocked out even a tiny patch of sky. It was as though we were in a deep green bubble. A bubble that smelled like rot.

Then ruined buildings began to appear, suddenly rising out of the luxuriant growth. Part of a column. A statue with no arms or torso. Some sort of archway. Vines twisted around the decaying stone, and tendrils drifted across the grass like fingers clutching at our feet.

We arrived at a clearing filled with refugees. At one end was a large, ruined temple covered with vines and moss. Massive statues looked as though they had once supported the roof. Now there was no roof, and the statues were broken and lay on the ground. A large stone eye gave me a hostile stare.

It was all so strange and eerie. The Gungans looked at us with angry eyes. Had I led us into a trap?

I had made a decision based on desperate need, but also on how I felt about Jar Jar. He was decent and good. But what about his people? He could be the exception rather than the rule.

A stout Gungan walked out, flanked by officers.

"Boss Nass," Jar Jar whispered to the Queen.

I had coached Sabé on board the transport. I had told her exactly what to say, and how to say it.

She stepped forward. "I am Queen Amidala of the Naboo," she said in a clear voice. "I come in peace."

Boss Nass did not look friendly. "Naboo biggen," he boomed angrily. "Youse da ones who bring Mackineeks. Yousa just as bombad as dey are. Yousa all die'n, mesa think."

Captain Panaka and the Naboo guards and pilots stiffened. The Jedi held themselves as casually as they always did. Even when the Gungans pointed their electropoles at us.

Not a good start. Boss Nass was contemptuous of the Queen in her rich robes. I saw the glint of fury in his eyes. To him, Queen Amidala was just as guilty as the Federation for the harm that had come to his people.

Speak, Sabé! Try again!

"I wish to form an alliance. . . ." Sabé began.

It would not work. I knew it, felt it in a flash of

insight. Sabé could do so many things as Queen. She couldn't do this.

Amidala couldn't sway Boss Nass, either. Padmé couldn't do it.

They both had to do it.

I'd have to strip away my last defense. Reveal my biggest secret.

I can't! I thought. My secret was the source of any power I had left. What would I be without it? What if by revealing who I was, I ended up failing my people? What if, by staying silent, I lost my last, best chance? Under my tunic, I felt Anakin's japor pendant against my skin. Maybe it was a symbol of a new power I would achieve. The power of truth.

My knees were shaking as I stepped forward. "*I* am Queen Amidala."

Somehow I'd expected that exposing my secret would create a vacuum inside me, and fear would rush in. But that didn't happen. I felt *satisfied*. The two parts of me came together. I could almost hear the resounding *click* as the two contradictions became a whole.

"Sabé is my decoy and protection," I said.

I heard Artoo beep softly behind me. Anakin looked at me in disbelief.

We are still the same, my eyes told him. He looked down at the ground.

Boss Nass sniffed suspiciously. The Gungans didn't lower their electropoles.

"I'm sorry for my deception," I said. "It was necessary. Although we have not always agreed, our two great societies have lived side by side in peace for generations. The Trade Federation has destroyed your world and mine. You are in hiding. My people are in camps. If we do not act together, all will be lost forever. I ask you to help us, Your Honor."

I had not won him over. He stood, legs apart, unmoved. What could I do to convince him?

"I beg you to help us," I said. I dropped to my knees before him.

Captain Panaka and his troops gasped. I knew what they were thinking. A Naboo kneeling before a Gungan! Well, they would kneel, too. What did this invasion tell us but that all of the people of Naboo had to stand shoulder to shoulder and fight as equals?

"We are all your humble servants, Boss Nass. Our fate is in your hands," I said.

Slowly, one by one, they knelt. Finally, the Jedi knelt, too.

The silence pressed against my ears. Even the chattering birds were quiet. It seemed an eternity before I heard an odd, chugging sound.

Boss Nass was laughing.

"Yousa no tinken yousa greater den da Gungans! Mesa like this. Maybe wesa bein friends."

And thus, the great alliance of the Gungans and the Naboo was formed.

Now, for the battle.

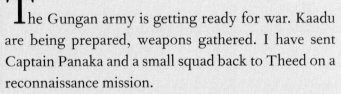

The Gungan army is getting ready for war. Kaadu are being prepared, weapons gathered. I have sent Captain Panaka and a small squad back to Theed on a reconnaissance mission.

Boss Nass has brought us to the grasslands surrounding the swamp. Here is where the great battle will be launched. Here is where we wait for Panaka's return. Everything depends on his getting close enough to Theed to gather information.

LATER

Panaka is back. His mission was successful. He has reported that most of the people are in camps, as we knew. But a few officers and guards have maintained an underground resistance movement. He brought back as many leaders as he could find.

He added that the Federation army was much larger than we'd thought. "This is a battle we cannot win," he told me gravely.

It was time to reveal my plan at last. We don't need to win the battle. It is only a diversion. While the Gungans draw the droid army away from Theed, we'll enter the city through the secret passages by the waterfalls. Once we reach the palace, Captain Panaka will create a diversion. A small squad of us will enter the palace and capture the viceroy. Without him, the droids will be lost and confused.

I asked Qui-Gon what he thought of the plan. I'm not afraid anymore of seeming weak if I ask for advice.

He looked thoughtful. "The viceroy will be well guarded."

I could see Captain Panaka's military mind working. He lives on our peaceful planet, but he's well trained in military tactics.

"The real difficulty is getting into the throne

room," he said. "Once we're inside, we shouldn't have a problem."

Qui-Gon turned to Boss Nass and told him that there was a possibility that many Gungans would be killed.

Boss Nass nodded. He was ready for that.

I had considered this, too. I didn't want Naboo's freedom to be on the backs of slaughtered Gungans. I volunteered our pilots to immobilize the droid army by knocking out the Droid Control Ship orbiting the planet. If we could get beyond their ray shields and knock out communications, the droids would be helpless. The droids cannot think for themselves — if we destroy the Control Ship, they will be paralyzed.

Did I spy a flicker of approval on Qui-Gon's rugged face?

"A well-conceived plan," he said. "But there is great risk. The weapons on your fighters may not penetrate the shields."

Obi-Wan spoke for the first time. "There is a greater danger. If the viceroy escapes, Your Highness, he'll return with another droid army. And I'm certain he will show no mercy."

A chill ran through me. They were right.

"That is why we must not fail to get the viceroy," I said. "Everything depends on that."

We leave for Theed in an hour.

LATER

I know the route through the waterfalls well. We reached the plaza without being seen. Battle droids and tanks were clustered in the wide square.

"We'll split up here," Panaka said in a low tone. "I'll keep a squad on this side and create a diversion. Your Highness, your group will head for the main hangar. We've got to get those pilots in the air."

I nodded. Qui-Gon, Obi-Wan, Anakin, Artoo, Eirtaé, and I headed for the hangar. Sabé, still in royal dress, stayed with Panaka's squad.

It felt so strange to creep around the plaza I had once strolled across so freely. Now I crouched, blaster in hand, ready to do whatever I had to.

We heard the sound of blaster fire behind us. Panaka had begun the diversion.

Qui-Gon urged me to hurry.

When we burst into the hangar, we received immediate fire from the battle droids. Qui-Gon and Obi-Wan deflected the laser fire with their lightsabers. I threw myself behind a wall and looked around anxiously for Anakin. He was crouched behind a fighter. Safe for the moment.

I took aim at a battle droid and fired. I have been trained in weapons handling, but it was the first time I'd aimed at an enemy. The battle droid went down.

My instincts kicked in. With the Jedi beside me, I wasn't afraid.

I called to the pilots to get to the ships. Two pilots were able to take off. But the droids were able to position a tank to blast them with laser cannon. One of the ships exploded.

But one got through.

Captain Panaka burst into the hangar, blasting laser fire. The last of the droids went down. More pilots rushed to the remaining ships.

"We've got to get to the palace!" I called to Qui-Gon. He nodded.

He turned to where Anakin was hiding behind a Naboo fighter. "Stay here, Annie!" he shouted.

We began to run toward the exit. But before we reached it, a dark-cloaked figure filled the opening. He did not reach for a weapon. He just stood there.

His evil aura invaded the hangar like a creeping, foul mist. It was the dark warrior who had fought Qui-Gon on Tatooine. The one who almost destroyed him.

"We'll handle this," Qui-Gon said tersely.

I felt fear for the first time that day. "No," I whispered.

His eyes met mine for a brief moment. That vivid blue sent me his thoughts, as clear as if he'd spoken them.

This is how it must be. You have your own part to play. Go.

I didn't want to leave him. But I obeyed him, one last time. I ran out of the hangar with Captain Panaka, my handmaidens, and the rest of the Naboo soldiers.

I headed for the palace. And I left Qui-Gon behind.

The palace entrances were heavily guarded by battle droids. It would be suicide to attempt to enter that way. Plus it would be better to invade as near to the throne room as we could.

We hurried to the side of the palace that overlooked the waterfall. The sound of rushing water thundered in our ears, and I felt the spray on my face. Captain Panaka and some of his soldiers shot out cables that hooked onto a high ledge.

We scaled the exterior wall of the palace. Captain Panaka blasted out a window. We swung inside. The throne room was only a few feet away.

"Everyone stay together," Panaka warned. I exchanged a look with Sabé, and she drifted toward the rear of the group. It was the only part of the plan I'd kept secret from the others. I took a position next to Panaka.

Suddenly, destroyer droids appeared in front of the throne room doorway. Their blasters were pointed directly at us. We looked to the other end of the hall. Another group of destroyer droids appeared.

Trapped!

"Throw down your weapons," I said. I let my blaster fall from my hand. It clattered on the ground. "They've won this round."

Captain Panaka stared at me, incredulous. I ordered him and his officers to throw down their weapons. Reluctantly, they did.

The droids surrounded us. They brought us into the throne room, where Nute Gunray was waiting. He stared for a long moment at me, and I met his gaze coolly. I saw the start of recognition in his eyes. And then the contempt.

"Your little insurrection has failed, Your Highness," he said to me, using my title like an insult. "It's time for you to sign the treaty."

From behind me, I heard Sabé's voice.

"I will not sign any treaty, Viceroy. Because you have lost!"

Nute did a double take. The Neimoidian guards looked from Sabé to me and back again. Before they could react, Sabé turned and fled.

"After her!" Nute screamed to the guards. "This one is a decoy! Get the Queen!"

Six of the droids rushed out after Sabé. Our odds were improving.

"Your Queen will not get away with this," Nute hissed to me.

I staggered back, as if defeat had dissolved my muscles. I slumped down onto the throne behind me. While I pretended to be overcome, my fingers frantically searched for a hidden security button.

I found it! A panel in my desk slid open silently. A cache of blasters was concealed there. Although Naboo had discouraged weapons, it was deemed that the Queen would need a last line of defense. The blasters were kept in perfect working condition.

I tossed one to Panaka, and one to his first officer. Then I blasted the last battle droid. I activated the security throne room door, which slid shut. Panaka's officer jammed the controls near the door.

I leveled my blaster at Nute while I tossed more pistols to the Naboo officers.

"Now," I said, "I think it's time we renegotiated, Viceroy."

Nute laughed. "Don't be absurd. You're still outnumbered. Battle droids will blast through that door in minutes."

I settled myself back on the throne and kept the blaster aimed at his chest. "We shall see."

"This would be amusing if it weren't so pathetic," Nute said. "Come, come, Your Highness. You are playing at war like a child. I have an *army* out there."

"And I have a blaster leveled at your chest," I said calmly.

He looked a little nervous. "Now, I didn't say we couldn't negotiate. The treaty —"

He was interrupted by the sound of droids blasting at the door outside. His expression cleared, and he smiled. "There. A word from me either way, and they will cut you in two or spare you, Your Highness. Your choice."

The door shook under pressure. Panaka gave me a slightly nervous glance. Another laser blow caused the hinge to melt.

"You see —" Nute began. He stopped. All was silent outside in the hallway.

"What —" Nute stared at the door as though it could talk. "Keep blasting, you idiots!"

Hope leaped in my chest. I leaned over and punched up the view screen.

The lead Naboo pilot appeared. He looked exhausted. Triumphant. "We did it. Mission accomplished, Your Highness. Look!"

The cockpit camera was now trained on the burning hulk that used to be the Droid Control Ship. The cheers of the pilots resounded through the throne room. I closed my eyes for a moment. Naboo was free. The battle droids had all shut down. When I opened my eyes again, Panaka was grinning at me.

"It's impossible," Nute whispered. His voice rose to a whine. "Impossible!"

I reached over to the desk and picked up the treaty. I tore it in two and flung the pieces in his face. "There is your treaty, Viceroy! Sorry I can't sign it."

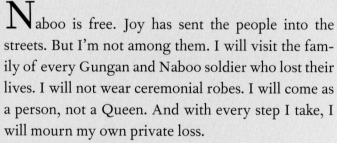

Naboo is free. Joy has sent the people into the streets. But I'm not among them. I will visit the family of every Gungan and Naboo soldier who lost their lives. I will not wear ceremonial robes. I will come as a person, not a Queen. And with every step I take, I will mourn my own private loss.

Qui-Gon is dead.

He died bravely. Of course he died bravely. Obi-Wan told me the details. How they fought Darth Maul down into the bowels of the power generator next door to the hangar. How Qui-Gon came back again and again to strike the dark warrior. But it was Qui-Gon who took the killing blow. It was left to Obi-Wan to kill Darth Maul.

It was hard for Obi-Wan to tell me these things. I will always value his kindness in coming to see me, knowing I would want to hear about the terrible event from him.

Anakin suffers. In the midst of my sadness, I am proud of him. He bears his sorrow bravely. Anakin is the hero of the great battle for Naboo. I was shocked to hear that it was he who struck the Federation ship and annihilated it. He had never piloted a fighter before, only a Podracer. Yet he flew into space, to the Federation ship, directly into its hangar, and blew its reactor.

Well. Maybe I'm not so surprised after all.

Today is a day for mourning. I must stop now. Today, we celebrate Qui-Gon's life.

THE NEXT DAY

Qui-Gon's funeral was attended by many Jedi Masters and as many people of Naboo that could crowd into the plaza. Afterward, I went to see Obi-Wan.

The people have called for a victory parade, and one has been scheduled. I wanted to call it off. A joyous parade felt wrong, with Qui-Gon gone.

Obi-Wan's face was etched with sadness. Qui-

Gon's death has affected him deeply. But he seemed to soften as he took in my grief.

"Qui-Gon was a Jedi Master," he said. "Which means he was a serious man. Maybe you even found him — a little too solemn at times?"

I smiled through my tears. "At times."

"What you may not know is that he not only valued celebration, he enjoyed it," Obi-Wan said. "He believed in your cause, Your Highness. He would want you to march at the head of that victory parade. And he would want you to enjoy every minute of it."

I thought about Obi-Wan's words. Finally, I nodded. "Then I will go. But only if you ride beside me. It's your victory, too. Yours and Qui-Gon's."

Obi-Wan considered this. "If you wish it, Your Highness," he said slowly, "then I shall be honored."

"Then we'll celebrate his victory tomorrow," I agreed softly. "And we will mourn his loss forever."

CELEBRATION

Children threw flowers, and Gungan and Naboo marched side by side. The streets are full of singing and laughter again.

Palpatine joined us for the parade. He has been appointed Supreme Chancellor. I hope that this position will ensure Naboo's future.

Anakin has told me that he will study with Obi-

Wan as a Jedi apprentice. Apparently they are break-ing every rule for the boy. That's how much promise he shows.

Before the parade, Anakin and I snatched a private good-bye.

"I'll see you again," he promised me in that fierce, serious way he has.

I touched his cheek. "I have no doubt that you will," I told him. "Our fates are bound together, Anakin. That I know."

During the parade, I looked out over the cheering crowds of Gungans and Naboo. My beautiful emer-ald world is free. We have made peace. The camps have been demolished. The people have returned to their homes.

I turned to Obi-Wan. "I'm glad it's over," I told him. "I've gone to war, but I value this above all." I gestured at the crowd. "Peace."

"Peace is what we strive for," Obi-Wan agreed. "And I hope you will never have to do battle again. But I'm not sure how completely we can choose our fates."

Those Jedi and their wisdom! I'm smiling now, re-membering Qui-Gon. He had that same infuriating habit of being right.

Yes, Obi-Wan. I hate to admit it, but you're right. Who knows what lies ahead? Fate is a tangle. We can only follow a thread.

The epic begins . . .

EPISODE I
THE PHANTOM MENACE™
By Patricia C. Wrede
Based on the screenplay and story by George Lucas

See Episode I through their eyes . . .

EPISODE I
JOURNAL

Anakin Skywalker
Queen Amidala

. . . and more to come

Before there was *The Phantom Menace*, there was . . .

JEDI APPRENTICE

#1 The Rising Force

#2 The Dark Rival

. . . and more to come